CARTOON
NETWORK™

SCOOBY-DOO!
MAP IN THE MYSTERY MACHINE

Look for the **SCOOBY DOO READERS**
Collect them all!

#**1** The Map in the Mystery Machine

#**2** Disappearing Donuts

Coming soon:

#**3** Howling at the Playground

By Gail Herman

Illustrated by Duendes del Sur

SCHOLASTIC INC.

New York Toronto London Auckland Sydney
Mexico City New Delhi Hong Kong

No part of this work may be reproduced, stored in a retrieval system, or transmitted in any form or by any means, electronic, mechanical, photocopying, recording, or otherwise, without written permission of the publisher. For information regarding permission, write to Scholastic Inc., Attention: Permissions Department, 555 Broadway, New York, NY 10012.

ISBN 0-439-16167-3

40 39 38   40   15 16/0

Designed by Mary Hall

Printed in the U.S.A.
First Scholastic printing, March 2000

Scooby-Doo and his friends left Vinny's Pizza.

Velma, Fred, and Daphne waved good-bye to Vinny and his nephew, Joe.

Beep!

A delivery truck whizzed by.

Scooby dove under the Mystery Machine.

"Rook!" he cried.

"It's a map!" Velma said.

The map was old and torn.

"It looks like a mystery," Fred said.

"It looks like an old pirate's map!" Velma said.

"Maybe the map will lead to a buried treasure!" said Daphne.

"Like, maybe we should not mess with a pirate's ghost," Shaggy said.

"Come on, gang!" Fred said. "We should check this out."

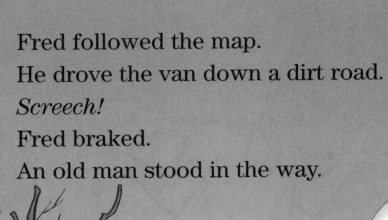

Fred followed the map.

He drove the van down a dirt road.

Screech!

Fred braked.

An old man stood in the way.

"Do not enter here!" the man shouted.
"This road is haunted! Turn back!"
"Good idea!" said Shaggy. "Let's go."
"Reah!" barked Scooby.
"Not so fast," Fred said.

Daphne and Fred and Velma wanted to explore.

"Let's split up," said Fred.

Shaggy and Scooby looked at each other.
To the left, the road was not so dark.
"Scooby and I will go left," Shaggy said.

Shaggy and Scooby took two steps.

"I think that's far enough," Shaggy said.
Then he cried, "Zoinks!"

Right in front of them stood a ghost.
"Ahhh!" shouted Shaggy.
"Rahhh!" shouted Scooby.

They raced down the road.
And there, up ahead, was a building.
A safe place!
Shaggy and Scooby dashed inside.

Scooby sniffed and grinned.
Shaggy's stomach rumbled.
It was a pizza kitchen!

"Rizza!" said Scooby.

What luck!

Scooby and Shaggy went to work —
rolling, tossing, slicing, dicing.

Pizza with everything on top — and
everything all over!
Scooby threw the dough.
Up, down. Up, down, and . . .

"Roops!" said Scooby. "Rorry!"
The dough landed on Velma's head!
"What are you guys doing here?"
asked Shaggy.

"We followed the map," Daphne told him.
"It *is* a treasure map," Fred said.
"It is an ad for the Pizza Treasure
Restaurant," Velma said.

"That's one mystery solved!" said Shaggy. "But what about the other one?"

"The other one?" said Velma.

"The rhost!" Scooby cried.

"We saw it near the van," Shaggy explained.

"Hmmm," Velma said. "A ghost."
She took out a napkin.
"I found this on the road — right by the Mystery Machine. I have a hunch about this ghost."

"Time to set a trap!" said Fred.

Everyone turned to Scooby and Shaggy.

Scooby gulped.

"You want *us* to be the trap?" asked Shaggy.

Velma nodded.

"Ro way!" said Scooby.

"Not even for a Scooby Snack?" Daphne asked.

Scooby shook his head.

"What about two Scooby Snacks?" Velma asked.

"Rokay!" Scooby-Doo said.

Scooby and Shaggy walked down the spooky road.

"Scooby treats are just the beginning!" Shaggy told Scooby. "Soon we'll be eating pizza at Pizza Treasure!"

"Wooh!"

Zoinks! It was the ghost!

Scooby jumped into Shaggy's arms.
"Like, let's get out of here!" said
Shaggy.
In a flash, they raced away.
But the ghost was right behind them!

All at once, Shaggy tripped.

Bump! Scooby fell right on the ghost!

"Scooby-Dooby-Doo!" Scooby barked.

Velma, Fred, and Daphne ran over to see what happened.

"The costume party is over, ghost,"
said Velma.

Fred tore off the mask.

It was Joe, Vinny's nephew from
Vinny's Pizza!

"He's scaring people from this road," Fred explained. "Just like that old man said."

"He does not want anyone to go to Pizza Treasure," Daphne said.

"The napkin gave me the first clue," Velma added.

Shaggy looked at Joe, surprised.

"But, like, the pizza at Vinny's is great. We will never stop going there!"

"Really?" said Joe.

"Reah!" said Scooby.

"It is good to have two pizza places in town," Fred said.

"Like, then we can have a double order at two places," Shaggy said. He rubbed his rumbling stomach.

"Reah!" Scooby agreed. The gang followed Joe to Vinny's Pizza for an extra special pizza party.